P9-CTA-864

TiGER CAN'T SLEEP

by **S. J. Fore**

illustrated by **R. W. Alley**

ViKING

To my mother and father, for their lifelong encouragement and support.
And with eternal gratitude to my editor, Janet B. Pascal.—S.J.F.

For Aunt Norma, who has many closets, all equally fun.—R.W.A.

VIKING
Published by Penguin Group

Penguin Young Readers Group, 345 Hudson Street, New York, New York 10014, U.S.A.
Penguin Group (Canada), 90 Eglinton Avenue East, Suite 700, Toronto, Ontario, Canada M4P 2Y3
(a division of Pearson Penguin Canada Inc.)
Penguin Books Ltd, 80 Strand, London WC2R 0RL, England
Penguin Ireland, 25 St Stephen's Green, Dublin 2, Ireland (a division of Penguin Books Ltd)
Penguin Group (Australia), 250 Camberwell Road, Camberwell, Victoria 3124, Australia
(a division of Pearson Australia Group Pty Ltd)
Penguin Books India Pvt Ltd, 11 Community Centre, Panchsheel Park, New Delhi – 110 017, India
Penguin Group (NZ), Cnr Airborne and Rosedale Roads, Albany, Auckland 1310, New Zealand
(a division of Pearson New Zealand Ltd)
Penguin Books (South Africa) (Pty) Ltd, 24 Sturdee Avenue, Rosebank, Johannesburg 2196, South Africa

Penguin Books Ltd, Registered Offices: 80 Strand, London WC2R 0RL, England

First published in 2006 by Viking, a division of Penguin Young Readers Group

1 3 5 7 9 10 8 6 4 2

Text copyright © S. J. Fore, 2006
Illustrations copyright © R. W. Alley, 2006

LIBRARY OF CONGRESS CATALOGING-IN-PUBLICATION DATA
Fore, S. J.
Tiger can't sleep / by S. J. Fore ; illustrations by R. W. Alley.
p. cm.
Summary: A young boy is kept awake by the noisy, "talented" tiger
in his closet that is busy dancing, eating, and making music.
ISBN 0-670-06078-X (hardcover)
[1. Bedtime—Fiction. 2. Tigers—Fiction. 3. Fear of the dark—Fiction.]
I. Title: Tiger cannot sleep. II. Alley, R. W. (Robert W.), ill. III. Title.
PZ7.F75812Tig 2006   [E]—dc22   2005017734

Manufactured in China
Set in Typeka
Book design by Nancy Brennan

Cozy bed . . . time to sleep.

But I **can't** sleep because there's a tiger in my closet . . .

... a tiger in my closet
eating potato chips!

I don't hear any crunch-crunch-crunching.

I don't hear any bounce-bounce-bouncing.

I don't hear any ker-thump-thump, ouching.

I don't hear any tap-tap-tap-tapping.

I don't hear any oom-pah, oom-pahing.

I don't hear any boom-boom-boom-crashing.

I don't hear any click-clack, click-clacking.

I don't even hear any boo-hoo-hooing.

Everything is quiet.

Now I'll finally be able to sleep!

Suddenly I hear a noise coming from under the covers.

It gets louder and louder...

and louder.

I can't sleep
because there's a
tiger snoring in my bed.